Bikes at Work

Written by Brylee Gibson

Rigby

People can have bikes for work.

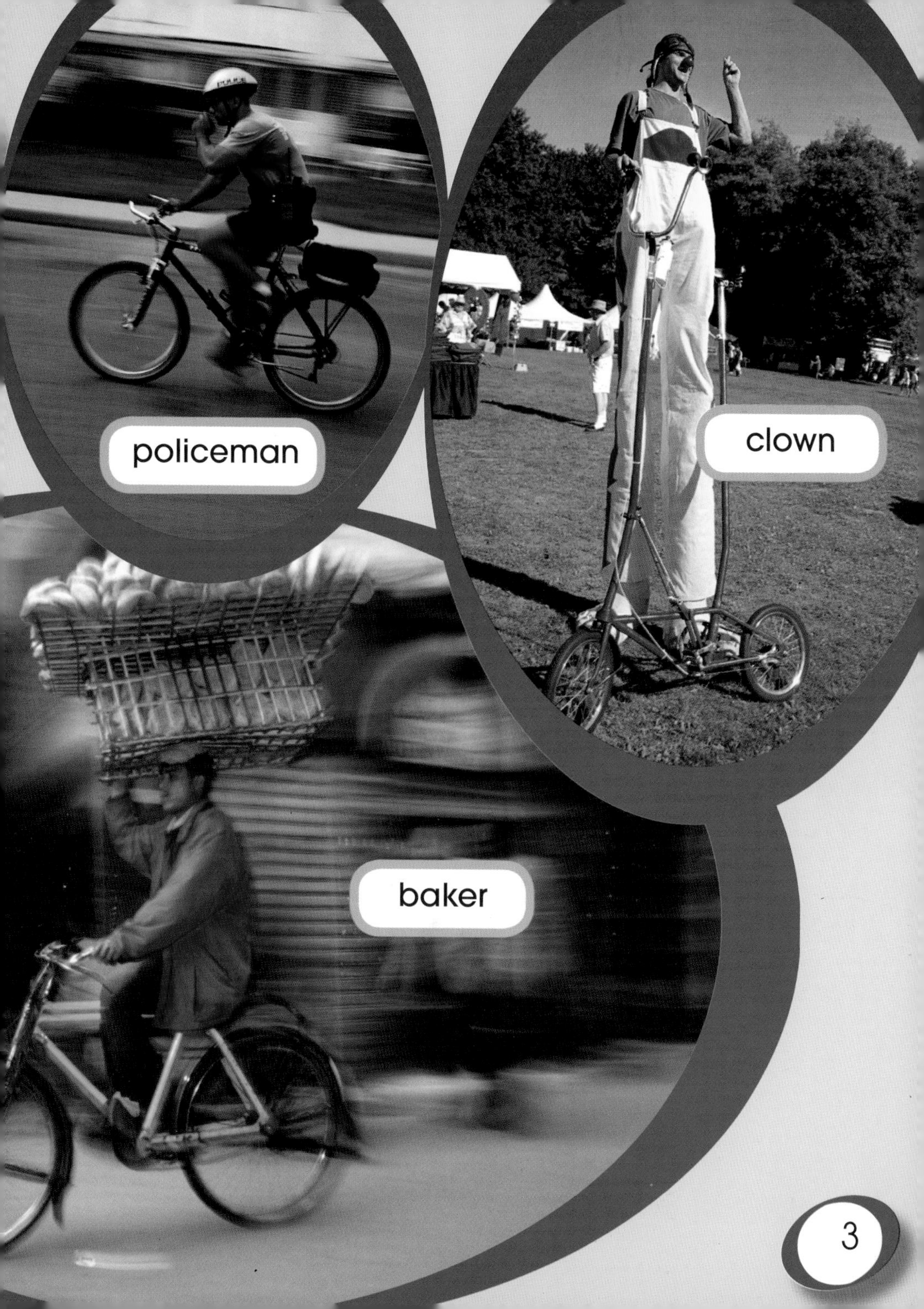
policeman
clown
baker

This man is
on his bike.

He will get
the sheep.

People are
on the bike.
They are going
for a ride.

A box is on this bike.
The box is
for ice cream.
A woman is
on the bike, too.

Super Star
Marino's ITALIAN
ICES
OLD TIME FAVORITE
TWIN POP

Look at this bike.
The man is **not**
on his bike.
The bananas are
on his bike.

bananas

Look at this bike.
This bike is for
a clown.

clown

Look at the bikes.
A bike for food.
A bike for flowers.
And a bike for bread!

Index

Guide Notes

Title: Bikes at Work
Stage: Early (2) – Yellow

Genre: Nonfiction
Approach: Guided Reading
Processes: Thinking Critically, Exploring Language, Processing Information
Written and Visual Focus: Photographs (static images), Index, Labels
Word Count: 92

Thinking Critically

(sample questions)

- Look at the title and read it to the children. Ask the children what they think this book might be about.
- Focus the children's attention on the index. Ask: "What are you going to find out about in this book?"
- If you want to find out about a bike for a clown, which page would you look on?
- If you want to find out about a bike for bread, which page would you look on?
- What is different about the way the bike is used on pages 4 and 5 and the way the bike is used on pages 10 and 11?
- Why do you think bikes might be used for work?

Exploring Language

Terminology

Title, cover, photographs, author, photographers

Vocabulary

Interest words: people, ride, bananas, clown
High-frequency words: his, get
Positional word: on

Print Conventions

Capital letter for sentence beginnings, periods, comma, exclamation mark